Planting More Than Pansies
A Fable about Love

Written by Stacey Bess

Illustrated by Melissa Ricks

SHADOW
MOUNTAIN

SALT LAKE CITY, UTAH

Text © 2003 Stacey Bess
Illustrations © 2003 Melissa Ricks

Shadow Mountain is a registered trademark of Deseret Book Company.

Visit us at deseretbook.com

Library of Congress Cataloging-in-Publication Data
Bess, Stacey.
    Planting more than pansies : a fable about love / written by Stacey Bess ; illustrated by Melissa Ricks.
      p. cm.
    Summary: A father teaches his daughter that planting pansies is like raising children: they both need
      protection, nourishment, and faith if they are to flourish.
    ISBN 1-57008-893-4 (alk. paper)
      1. Gardening—Fiction. 2. Fathers and daughters—Fiction. 3. Faith—Fiction. I. Ricks, Melissa.
    II. Title.
PZ7.B46545Pl   2003
[E]—dc21
                                2002153941

Printed in China
Palace Press International, Hong Kong
                                 68875-7020

10   9   8   7   6   5   4   3   2   1

To my husband, Greg, who truly understands the wisdom of the Master Gardener. Special thanks also to Annette Haws for believing that this story should be told and for guiding me through the process
—SB

For my supportive husband, Boyd
—MR

"addy, is it my turn to help?" Sarah was bent so close to the hole her father had dug, he could have planted her nose.

"Almost," he said as he lifted a periwinkle pansy from a flat of tiny flowers. He laid the little plant carefully in the ground, firmed the earth around its roots, then reached for his trowel to dig another hole.

The neighbors driving by shook their heads.

"Those pansies will get snowed on in a week," one said.

"You'd better check your calendar," said another. "You're supposed to plant flowers in the SPRING!"

Dad looked at Sarah and winked. He knew better. He had planted pansies every fall for years and years. It was a family tradition—one of their oldest, and one of their best.

"Daddy," Sarah begged again, "is it my turn to plant a pansy?"

"You're right," he said. "It's exactly time for you to plant a pansy." He handed her a small blue flower and guided the pudgy hand.

"We have to be careful that we don't bruise the leaves," he said. "Pansies are like little girls: they're very pretty, but they can get hurt if we're not gentle."

Sarah nodded at her father as she gently tucked the little plant into the hole. She stroked a velvety petal with her finger while her father shared the secrets for growing perfect pansies—secrets that he had learned from the Master Gardener.

I t takes faith to plant pansies in the fall, when the storms are on their way. But if you nurture and love them and help them take root, the harsh winter won't hurt them, and in the spring when the snow melts, you'll see magic." He smiled at his little girl. "When all the neighbors have plain, brown flower beds, we'll have bright blue periwinkle pansies." He helped Sarah finish planting her flower, then placed his finger under her chin and looked into her face.

"Now you're part of the magic of our pansy patch."

Sarah was pleased. She straightened her back and tried to sound like a real gardener.

"Why do you plant the pansies so close together? I think you should put them all over the garden, like polka-dots," she said.

Her father turned to her so their knees touched. "The pansies have to make it through the winter and bad weather, and that's a tough job for a pansy to do alone. We plant them close together so their roots can intertwine; that way they can help each other through the storms and cold. The pansies are like a family, holding hands so that nobody falls down."

Sarah watched as he poured mulch from a burlap bag and worked it into the soil around the tender plants.

"The mulch is like a warm blanket they can lie under during the icy storms," he explained.

"Daddy, could they die?"

"Storms and cold are hard on young plants, but I have faith they'll make it if we give them what they need—food and water and a blanket." He picked up a handful of mulch and let it fall on the blossoms below.

"And love," Sarah said with a big smile.

"And love," Dad grinned back.

"Daddy, is faith magic?"

"Well," he said, brushing a smudge of dirt off her knee, "faith is when you believe in someone or something enough that you let it go, so it can become what it was meant to be. We could leave the pansies in their box and keep them inside where it's always warm, but eventually they'd be cramped and run out of room to grow, and they wouldn't fill this patch with flowers. I have faith that if we plant the pansies now, they'll blossom in the spring, just like I have faith that you'll bloom into a beautiful young woman with periwinkle pansies in your hair."

Sarah laughed as she imagined herself with flowers growing in her hair, while her father finished planting the last tiny flower on the last golden day of Indian summer.

Dressed in her flannel pajamas, Sarah pressed her nose against the cold glass of the window, wanting the long, dark winter to end. On this particular day, Sarah wasn't feeling too hopeful. The weatherman had predicted a heavy snow, and Sarah watched as it fell and fell in frozen feathers. The wind whipped through the bare trees and piled the flakes in drifts along the sidewalk by the pansy patch. Sarah shivered, thinking of the little flowers under their blanket of mulch and snow.

addy came up from behind and caught her in his arms. "I see you every morning at the window in such deep thought. What are you thinking?"

"I'm thinking, I hope this horrible storm won't hurt my pansies."

Dad chuckled at his daughter's concern.

"Remember, we did the best that we could to help them. Now we have to have a little faith. Besides, it's only February. Those little flowers are tucked under their snowy blanket, waiting for the sunshine, just like you."

"Do you think they're missing me, Daddy, like I'm missing them?"

"Absolutely." Dad hugged her, then set her down and walked back into the warmth of the kitchen where Mom was preparing breakfast.

Sarah watched a few moments longer, then whispered to the tiny plants caught in the storm, "Hold hands, little pansies. Daddy says that spring will come again. I love you, little pansies. Be safe."

Spring and sunshine finally came. The heavy winter blanket slowly melted, and together, Dad and Sarah watched the magic as the young plants stretched toward the sun, growing stronger, larger, and more colorful. Surely, Dad and Sarah thought every year, this garden is the most magical of all, but each succeeding spring they were surprised as the flowers in the garden seemed more beautiful than they had ever been before. And with each new season, the father humbly thanked the Master Gardener for giving him wisdom to nurture periwinkle pansies . . . and beautiful little girls.

As Sarah watched the garden, season after season, her father watched her, his most precious flower, as she bloomed into a beautiful young girl, then young woman.

And as Sarah had worried over the pansy patch, he worried over his little girl. Had he taught her enough of life? Had he nurtured her sufficiently? Had he loved her enough? Were her own roots deep enough to weather the storms that would surely come? And did he have faith enough to let her leave the garden?

For, each year, it seemed, she spent less and less time at his side in the garden. Her growing season was a busy time, with friends and music, school and games, clothes to wear and places to go, and other places to be seen. So many things took his daughter's attention away from the pansy patch. Of course they still hugged in the hall and called to each other at night from their beds: "I love you more than all the periwinkle pansies in the garden!"

Then Sarah would close her eyes and dream about big-girl things.

Dad continued to plant, season after season, but when he looked out to the horizon, he could see storm clouds gathering. The music behind the closed bedroom door grew loud. The friends, strangers to her father, acted knowing and secretive. The clothes became garish. The schoolwork, of which his daughter had been so proud, became less important. As summer waned, he watched Sarah let go and leave the garden, hurrying off to try to bloom on her own.

She tried to stand alone, but the winds were too strong; the temperatures dropped too suddenly; and the cold rains turned to ice. In the face of the storm, she first wavered, then fell.

er father, who had been watching, dropped to his knees and pleaded with the Master Gardener for wisdom. "Please," he begged, "I have done the best that I knew how. What more can be done?" And in his heart he heard the whispered reply.

"Be still. You have nurtured well. Now it is you who must learn wisdom from the pansies."

Bracing himself against the winter wind, he made his way out on the frozen earth, where he gathered his child up in a blanket and carried her back into the warmth of the house. But would she ever bloom again? Was there love enough to bring back the magic?

The wind howled and shook the windows. Snow piled high against the house. Winter stretched and blew into March and April with no sign of spring. The father barely noticed, as all his skills from years in the garden were sorely tried. His hands, roughened from hard work, wiped tears from a daughter's cheeks. His voice, quiet and low, soothed the girl as he brushed her long, dark hair and shared stories of other gardens and the Master Gardener who loves all Creation. He walked the floors at night to the sound of her soft sobbing. His heart reached toward hers, and that reaching started to bring a bloom back into the face of his most precious flower.

onsumed by his concern, he did not notice that in the world outside, the season for planting flowers had passed. He did not care that the beautiful garden, which had been his pride, was barren and filled with weeds through the warm summer months. In the fall he did not see the concerned faces of his neighbors as they asked one another, "Where did all the pansies go?"

He did not notice until his daughter, with a new smile on her face, pointed out to him the emptiness of his garden. Then he smiled also, and a short time later, on a warm September afternoon, the father was once again kneeling in his garden, his hands and knees covered with dirt, a trowel and a flat of blue and yellow pansies at his side. Lovingly, he worked the mulch into the soil before gently tucking each young plant into its hole.

The father looked up as he heard Sarah's laughter. He laughed with her as they both gazed at the beautiful little grandchild smiling in her mother's arms. Little Anna, a bit of dirt smeared across her cheek, clutched a small pansy in her fat little fist. She wiggled loose and toddled across the sidewalk toward her grandfather.

Sarah whispered, "Dad, you need to teach Anna about your pansy patch."

He said quietly, "This is your garden, too. Why don't you show her how to plant a pansy?"

Kneeling in the warm soil with her daughter, and helping little Anna hold the trowel in her hand, Sarah spoke the words she had heard so many times, "Anna, little girls are like pansies . . ."

For Anna, this digging was only a game. But someday she would learn that along with sunshine, life brings winds and storms that can batter the most beautiful flowers. Someday she would discover for herself that to weather the storms, people, like pansies, need deep roots and hands to hold. Someday, she would learn for herself the wisdom of the Master Gardener.

Grandpa looked from Sarah back to little Anna, mother and daughter, knee to knee in the garden, and felt something that seemed like a sunrise in his heart. Then he went back to his work, spading the soil and carefully planting tender flowers on an autumn day when most leaves had turned from green to gold. For he knew, however long the winter, if you plant well, someday they'll come back.